RECYCLING DUMP

By Andrea Butler
Illustrated by Jan Spivey Gilchrist

GoodYearBooks

In go the cans
with a clink, clink, clink.

In go the bottles
with a clank, clank, clank.

In go the jugs
with a clunk, clunk, clunk.

In go the papers
with a thump, thump, thump.

Clink, clank,

clunk, thump.

Off goes the truck
to the recycling dump.